Note to parents, carers and teachers

Read it yourself is a series of modern stories, favourite characters and traditional tales written in a simple way for children who are learning to read. The books can be read independently or as part of a guided reading session.

Each book is carefully structured to include many high-frequency words vital for first reading. The sentences on each page are supported closely by pictures to help with understanding, and to offer lively details to talk about.

The books are graded into four levels that progressively introduce wider vocabulary and longer stories as a reader's ability and confidence grows.

Ideas for use

- Begin by looking through the book and talking about the pictures. Has your child heard this story before?

- Help your child with any words he does not know, either by helping him to sound them out or supplying them yourself.

- Developing readers can be concentrating so hard on the words that they sometimes don't fully grasp the meaning of what they're reading. Answering the puzzle questions on pages 30 and 31 will help with understanding.

For more information and advice on Read it yourself and book banding, visit **www.ladybird.com/readityourself**

Book Band 6

Level 2 is ideal for children who have received some reading instruction and can read short, simple sentences with help.

Special features:

Frequent repetition of main story words and phrases

Short, simple sentences

One day, Dom saw a little red egg. It was a little bit hot... and it glowed.

Dom hid the little red egg under his bed.

6

7

Large, clear type

Careful match between story and pictures

The next day, the egg hatched. A little red dragon hatched out. She was a little bit hot. And... she glowed.

"I will call you Glow," said Dom.

8

Educational Consultant: Geraldine Taylor
Book Banding Consultant: Kate Ruttle

A catalogue record for this book is available from the British Library

Published by Ladybird Books Ltd
80 Strand, London, WC2R 0RL
A Penguin Company

002

ISBN: 978-0-71819-470-3

Printed in China

Dom's Dragon

Written by Mandy Ross
Illustrated by Emma McCann

One day, Dom saw a little red egg. It was a little bit hot... and it glowed.

Dom hid the little red egg under his bed.

The next day, the egg hatched. A little red dragon hatched out. She was a little bit hot. And... she glowed.

"I will call you Glow," said Dom.

"You must hide under the bed," said Dom, "or I will have to tell the king about you."

That night, Dom's bed was nice and warm.

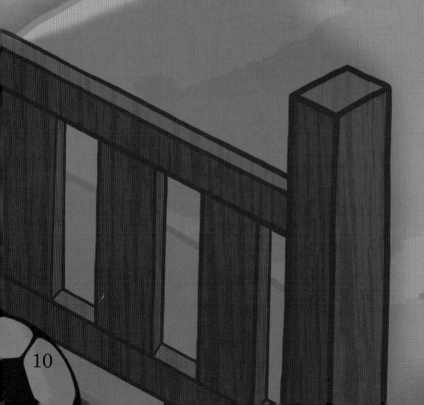

But Glow was growing
bigger and bigger.

"You must hide in the
bathroom," said Dom, "or
I will have to tell the king
about you."

The next day, there was very hot water in the bathroom. The towels were nice and warm, too.

But Glow was growing bigger and bigger.

"You must hide in the kitchen," said Dom, "or I will have to tell the king about you."

The next day there was nice hot food in the kitchen, on nice warm plates.

19

"Glow, you are getting too big and too hot," said Dom. "We will have to tell Mum."

"You have a dragon?" said Mum. "We will have to tell the king about her."

"You have a dragon?" said the king. "What will we do with her?"

"She has made everything nice and warm..." said Dom.

The king made a big house for Glow in the town. The house had very big pipes.

Dom took Glow to the house.

Glow made everything hot. The pipes took hot water to every house in the town. Everyone had nice warm towels, too.

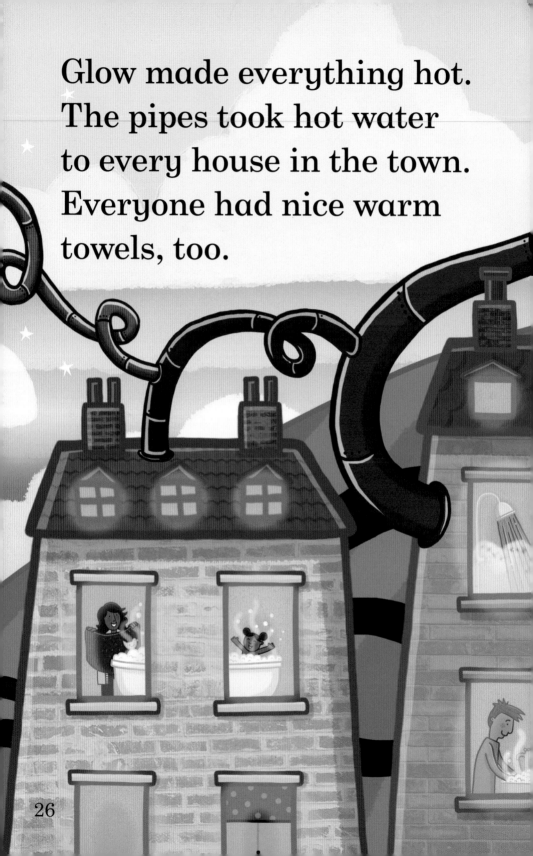

Glow made hot food for everyone in the town, on nice warm plates. Glow was happy. Dom was happy, too.

But one day, Dom saw three little red eggs...

How much do you remember about the story of Dom's Dragon? Answer these questions and find out!

- What colour is the little egg that Dom finds?

- Where does Dom first hide the dragon?

- Can you name two things that Glow makes nice and warm?

- What does the king make for Glow?

Look at the pictures and match them to the story words.

Dom

Glow

Mum

king

egg

Read it yourself with Ladybird

Tick the books you've read!

For beginner readers who can read short, simple sentences with help.

Level 2

Beauty and the Beast ☐

Chicken Licken ☐

Little Red Riding Hood ☐

Nature Trail ☐

Sports Day ☐

Pirate School ☐

Rumpelstiltskin ☐

Sleeping Beauty ☐

The Gingerbread Man ☐

Sly Fox and Red Hen ☐

The Tale of Jemima Puddle-Duck ☐

The Three Little Pigs ☐

Why Lion Roarrrs! ☐

The Big Race ☐

Town Mouse and Country Mouse ☐

Dom's Dragon ☐

For more confident readers who can read simple stories with help.

Level 3

YOU won't like this present as much as I DO! ☐

The Elves and the Shoemaker ☐

Hansel and Gretel ☐

Harry and the Bucketful of Dinosaurs ☐

Jack and the Beanstalk ☐

Furi on Music Island ☐

Poppet Stows Away ☐

Rapunzel ☐

The Red Knight ☐

Available on the App Store

The Read it yourself with Ladybird app is now available for iPad, iPhone and iPod touch

App also available on Android devices